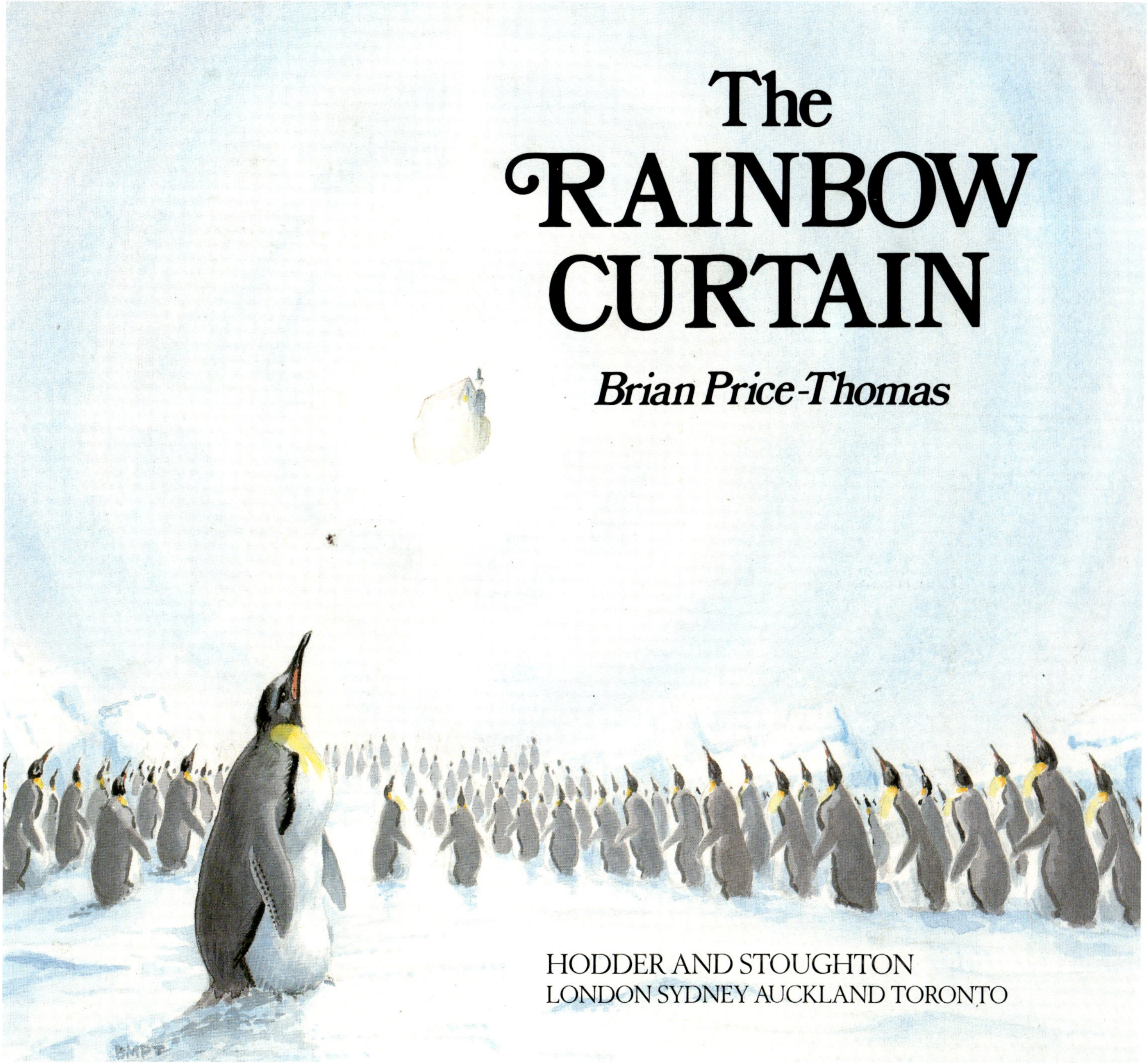

The RAINBOW CURTAIN

Brian Price-Thomas

HODDER AND STOUGHTON
LONDON SYDNEY AUCKLAND TORONTO

I think it must have been some time after Easter.

In the yard next door to our house, the workshop where Mr Antrobus made his wooden animals was locked with a big padlock.

The magic Noah's Ark, in which Mr Antrobus and I had flown all over the world, was not resting in the corner of the yard where it usually stood. All I saw was Nana's cat in the place where Mr Antrobus stored his wooden planks, and she was only hunting after mice.

"Has Mr Antrobus gone away?" I asked Nana.

"I've no more idea than the man in the moon. I'm far too busy looking after you and Grandad!" she said.

"How do people know what the man in the moon knows?" I asked.

Nana just laughed and went down to the vegetable garden to hang out the washing.

"The man in the moon might know," I said to Nana's cat which had followed me; but the cat just went on licking her paws.

"Well, he might anyway," I said to myself.

Before bedtime I liked to play on the floor by Grandad's chair, while Nana made things on her sewing machine.

"Nana says the man in the moon doesn't know if Mr Antrobus has gone away. What do you think, Grandad?"

"Why don't you try asking the man in the moon yourself?" Grandad replied.

"Don't put silly ideas in the boy's head just before bedtime," said Nana.

"There was a time when you used to make a wish to the new moon," smiled Grandad.

"That was quite different," said Nana, but she smiled too.

Perhaps it was the moonlight on my bedspread that woke me that night. I got up and opened the window wide.

"Do you know where Mr Antrobus is?" I whispered to the man in the moon, but he did not answer me.

I thought he would see me better in the garden, and there I could call more loudly without waking Nana and Grandad.

I lit my candle as Nana had taught me, and crept downstairs.

The grandfather clock seemed to be ticking very loudly in the hall.

"Hush, or you will wake Nana," I said.

In the kitchen, I put my candlestick on the table and blew out the candle before I opened the back door.

All was shadowy silver in the moonlight, and I walked down into the garden. As I did so, a bright light suddenly shone from Mr Antrobus's yard through the fence and across the garden to my feet.

I tiptoed along the golden-lit pathway, and there once more in the yard stood the Ark.

I saw that a light was shining from its nearly closed doors.

As I crossed the yard, the doors opened wide. A great brightness shone out from the Ark, filling the air all around me.

When my eyes had had a little time to get used to it, I saw the light was shaped as a great egg, which hung as if floating inside the Ark.

There by the door stood Mr Antrobus smiling at me, while on the bow of the Ark sat three white swans.

When I had climbed up beside Mr Antrobus, he closed the doors and, as had happened before when I had been with him, the ground moved away below us. It looked as soft as my bed feels just before I snuggle down to sleep.

Spreading their huge wings, the swans left the Ark to fly before us.
"Where are we going?" I asked.
"As far as the swans go, and then farther again," Mr Antrobus answered.
"How will we know when we have gone far enough?" I asked.
"Because we will have arrived," replied Mr Antrobus.
I did not ask any more because I knew that it would be so.

Time and the world passed by. All that seemed clear was the beating of the swans' white wings.

Then, just as I felt they must go on for ever, the swans turned in the sky and left us.

Mr Antrobus opened wide the doors of the Ark so that the bright light shone out, and below I saw the waves of an empty sea stretching all about us.

Like a lantern we hung still over the moving waters. I asked Mr Antrobus why we did so.

"Have patience, little one. We wait for the Great Whale," he replied.

So we waited.

After a time, Mr Antrobus turned to me and said,

"He comes to us now!"

It was as if I knew something huge was near, but I could not see it, and I was glad Mr Antrobus was beside me.

Then, in the same moment that Mr Antrobus raised his hat, the Great Whale's enormous head rose from the sea and everything else seemed very small.

All at once there appeared five dolphins jumping in and out of the waves around the Great Whale. I laughed because they were so beautiful.

Then Mr Antrobus waved his hand. Away went the Whale and the dolphins making a straight white bubbling pathway through the waves.

It seemed that the Ark was being drawn along above them, while the shining light of the egg showed the way.

Just as I was beginning to wonder if the journey would never end, I saw far, far away white shapes like ragged clothes on a long washing line.

"What are those?" I asked.

"Those are the icebergs that wander the cold seas of the South," Mr Antrobus replied.

As he spoke, the Whale and the dolphins leaped in the air before disappearing beneath the waves, leaving us to fly on alone between the frozen towers of ice.

Onwards went the Ark above the icebergs to a white land of snow.
    At last the world stood still below us, and I saw thousands of penguins standing looking up at us. I knew without asking that this place was the end of our journey.
    As I watched him, Mr Antrobus lifted the bright shining egg.
Holding it before him, he rose up
from the Ark and the egg lit
up the sky all around him.

As Mr Antrobus rose higher into the air, the egg seemed to become rainbow-coloured. Mr Antrobus stopped above me and opened his arms wide. He held one half of the egg in each hand.

The rainbow colours swirled out around him. Magic and silent, they spread across the sky, until the egg and its shell vanished away.

Then the Ark rose up towards Mr Antrobus and, when he was beside me again, I asked him, "Where has the egg gone?"

But Mr Antrobus did not answer.

Like a rainbow waterfall, the colours swirled across the sky. But they seemed always to move upwards.

"What is it?" I asked.

"It is the Aurora, the gift of the Sun to the long winter night of the South Pole," Mr Antrobus answered, and looking down on the land of the penguins, I saw that it was.

Then the Ark moved in towards the colours until the brightness streamed all about us.

When the Ark had passed through the coloured brightness, and we had set out on our journey home, I looked back for the last time. And I saw that the rainbow colours were hanging from the stars like a beautiful curtain.

"Will the Aurora stay there for ever?" I asked.

"Until the Sun himself comes to end the long winter night," Mr Antrobus answered.

"Was it really all in the egg?"

"Do you think that is important?"

I thought for a little while, then I said, "No, not so long as it is there."

And Mr Antrobus smiled down at me.

British Library Cataloguing in Publication Data
Price-Thomas, Brian
　　The rainbow curtain.
　　I. Title
　823'.914[J]　　PZ7
　ISBN 0-340-41569-X

Text and illustrations copyright © Brian Price-Thomas 1988

First published 1988

Published by Hodder and Stoughton Children's Books,
a division of Hodder and Stoughton Ltd,
Mill Road, Dunton Green, Sevenoaks, Kent TN13 2YJ

Printed in Great Britain by Cambus Litho, East Kilbride